Is There A Tiger Without Stripes

Shrika Pathipati

"I want to thank my Mummy, Daddy and
my little Brother Vikramaditya,
Thank you."

Autumn was a tiger that had
everything, but stripes.
She had the growl
of a tiger GROWL!!
& the bravery of the knight.

But,
her friends June, March
and Summer did not
see her as that type.
They saw her as a weak
little tiger with no stripes.

Autumn cried and cried all day and night.
She just wanted to be happy and bright.

So, she set out on a journey,
to figure out her tale and story!

On her way she found a
green frog,
who was busy catching flies
on a tree log.
He had a long tongue to catch a fly,
he catches one on his very first try.

"Mr.Frog, Mr.Frog, why don't I have stripes?",she asked him.
"You may not have stripes, but you can run as fast as the speed of light", replied the frog with a voice ever so grim.

Autumn was not happy with that answer,
she wanted one that would bring her laughter.

So, she set off again on her journey,
to find her real tale and story.

Not far from the frog, she found a small, brown mouse,
Who was cooking lunch in her small, green house
She was cooking such a small dish,
Which could not even fill a fish.

"Mrs.Mouse, Mrs.Mouse, why don't I have stripes?" she asked Mrs.Mouse.

"You may not have stripes, but you can hunt with might.", said Mrs.Mouse like she lived in the White House.

Autumn was not happy with that answer,
she wanted one that would make her happy faster.

So, she set off again
with a sad face on her
very own story's chase.

On her way,
she met a goofy monkey
Who was jumping
on a branch very lumpy.

He jumped near and
far just as crazy
as monkeys are.

"Mr.Monkey, Mr.Monkey, why don't I have stripes?" She asked him.
"You may not have stripes, but you are going to be the biggest cat in the world!", he said moving around in his monkey gym.

Walking home with her head down,
she had on her face a big fat frown.

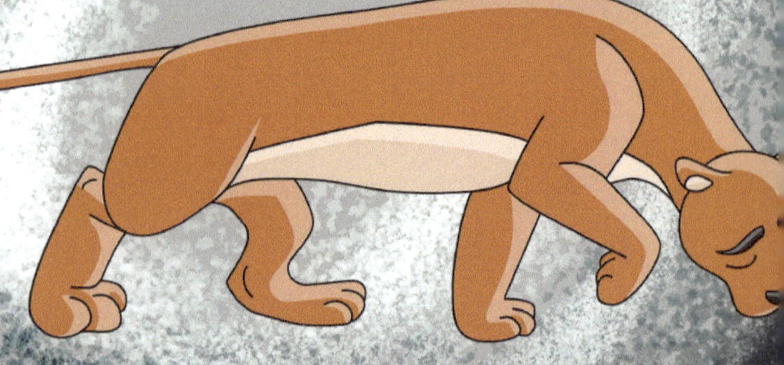

Walking and swirling was all she could do,
she never tried to see the good view;
the beautiful tiger she grew into.

Her mind thinking and thinking,
she couldn't get any idea to bling

She thought and thought about what the
animals had said,
All the thoughts dancing in her head.

You run as fast as light, one told her.
You hunt with might said another.
You're big and strong said the other.

Was this true, she thought to herself.
Am I a fast, brave and strong tiger
myself?

At home she beat the fellow cubs
in a race, but she still went
on her story's chase.
At home she hunts
with bravery and might.
But, the animal's
answers never
gave her
delight.

At home she looked
taller and greater
than her sisters
and brothers.
But, she still hid
behind her covers.

With a long face, she saw a tiger
through the corner of her eye
Moving around as time can fly

This tiger had no stripes on his body,
and was not like everybody,
He soared with might,
without a tiny sight of fright!

"How is your smile so wide?"
"When your Stripes have all dried?"
Autumn asks him,
When he gave her Smile so slim.
"I am unique an so are you",
"What others think, I have no clue,"
saying as he flew through.

A smile swooped through Autumn's face
as she ran through the land.
She just realized her pretty view,
making her free as sand.

Autumn looked at her body with pride,
As she ran across and watched herself glide.

The book smells of one main quality - self-esteem.
Self-esteem is one of those supreme qualities
that I'm trying to master during my teen years.
As the real world opens up every single day,
it's important that we mould ourselves with self-esteem.

It's a quality that cannot be achieved overnight,
but a lot of self-reflection
and hard work can be used as tools.
I have not mastered it myself,
but with this book and our morals,
we can do it together.

AUTHOR – Shrika Pathipati

I'm a 14-year-old aspiring innovator who wishes the best for the world!
Right now, I'm drilling my brain into biotech, especially in the sectors of longevity.
I want to introduce my ideas to young people who are keen on learning.
I've already made my first steps by writing this children's book
and performing as an Outreach Manager for the Beacon of Arts company.
I'm still on an unpredictable journey and my role in it is to make myself
the 'one' I want to be.

Illustrator – Mayur Khushal Gada

Mayur is an animator by profession with over 19 years of experience
and runs an youuutube channel in the name of "ChinuMeenu".
Very passionate about story telling and movies.